A Rather Remarkable Grizzly Bear

Marco
Master of Disguise

Praise for *Marco Moves In*:

'a compelling story'
Sunday Independent

'a madcap narrative'
Sunday Business Post

'illustrated with wonderful simplicity'
Roscommon Herald

Gerry Boland was born in Dublin but has lived in north Roscommon since 2001. He teaches creative writing in national schools in the area, works part-time in a local organic community garden, and spends as much time writing as he can. He is a commited environmentalist and an active campaigner on vegetarian and animal rights issues. His first collection of poems, *Watching Clouds*, was published by Doghouse Books in June 2011, and he is working on a collection of short stories. He is also the author of two travel books on Dublin.

Marco
Master of Disguise

Gerry Boland

Illustrated by Áine McGuinness

THE O'BRIEN PRESS
DUBLIN

First published 2012 by The O'Brien Press Ltd,
12 Terenure Road East, Rathgar, Dublin 6, Ireland.
Tel: +353 1 4923333; Fax: +353 1 4922777
E-mail: books@obrien.ie
Website: www.obrien.ie

ISBN: 978-1-84717-273-0

A catalogue record for this title is available from the British Library.

1 2 3 4 5 6 7 8 9
12 13 14 15 16

Layout and design: The O'Brien Press Ltd
Cover illustrations: Áine McGuinness

Printed in the Czech Republic by Finidr Ltd
The paper in this book is produced using pulp from
managed forests.

The O'Brien Press receives assistance from

Dedication

to Lisa, Kate and Gareth

Acknowledgements

Thanks are due to the following: Áine McGuinness for her inspired illustrations; everyone at The O'Brien Press; the Tyrone Guthrie Centre in Annaghmakerrig, where the first draft of *Marco Master of Disguise* was written; and as always, to Miriam

.

Marco
Master of Disguise

Nearly everyone in my class had a pet of some sort. Lots of them had dogs, and a few had cats, budgies and goldfish. Max Wallace had a hamster and Adam O'Hara had a tortoise which he claimed was sixty years old, though I'm pretty sure he was exaggerating. Sam Tripp had a small lizard *and* a pet rabbit, which was a strange combination.

But no one I knew had a grizzly bear sleeping in their garden shed, or sat beside a grizzly bear most nights watching TV.

Marco wasn't a pet, of course. He was my friend. My best friend.

Almost five months after Marco came knocking on our front door, looking for a cup of tea, the zoo was still searching for him. There were posters pasted up all over the city.

MISSING

GRIZZLY BEAR MISSING!!

If you see him contact the police immediately.

DO NOT APPROACH THE BEAR- HE IS VERY DANGEROUS!

I tore one of the posters off a pole at the top of our street and brought it home. I showed it to Marco.

'Is that me?'

'Who else could it be?'

'It looks like Rowdy.'

'Rowdy? Who's Rowdy?'

'He's my uncle. Last time I heard, he was in a zoo in Australia.'

'I think it's a photo of you, Marco. Look closely.'

He put his face up to the poster and his beautiful brown eyes gazed for a long time at the face of the bear looking back at him.

'Well,' I said, 'is it you, or is it Rowdy? All grizzly bears look the same to me.'

'It must be me. Rowdy has a scar over his right eye from a fight up in the Rockies, before they captured him. This face has no scar.'

The zoo was also offering a large reward for any information that would lead to Marco's capture. My main job was making sure that no one ever caught sight of him.

Mum was a great help. She was always on the lookout for anything that Marco could use as a disguise if someone called to the house.

Sometimes there wasn't time for him to put on a disguise. It was at times like these that Marco showed what a natural genius he was.

Like that June morning, right at the start of the school holidays, when five people called, one after the other. Mum had gone out for a few hours. Marco and I were watching TV and drinking a cup of tea, the two things Marco loved most.

We were watching a re-run of the final of the 1986 Superbowl, when the Chicago Bears trounced the New England Patriots 46-10.

Marco was a big Bears fan. He knew all the words of their fight song, *Bear Down, Chicago Bears.* I wouldn't let him sing it because he was the worst singer I ever heard. What came out of his mouth was a cross between a bear-type grunt and an elephant's snore.

The doorbell rang.

A man in a dark blue uniform stood on the doorstep.

'I'm here to read your meter,' he said.

I had no idea that Marco had paused the game and gone into the kitchen to boil more water. Luckily, he must have heard us coming through the hall, which gave him just enough time to slip out the back door but not enough time to get to the shed.

It was only when the meter man looked out the kitchen window that I realized what had happened.

'Is that a statue of the escaped grizzly bear?' he asked.

I walked over to the window and looked out.

Marco was crouched down on all fours on the tree stump in the middle of the garden. One paw was raised, as if he was about to strike out at a jumping fish. His body was stiff and tense and, apart from his fur, which was moving gently in the breeze, he was as still as a statue.

'It is,' I said.

'It's amazing. Who did it?'

'My mum. She makes statues in her spare time.'

'Can I have a closer look?'

'I'm afraid the door to the garden is jammed shut and can't be opened. You can go out and have a look the next time you read the meter.'

He took his mobile phone out of his pocket.

'That's the most incredible statue I've ever seen,' he said, as he took a few shots of Marco. 'Your mum is very talented. It looks exactly like the grizzly that escaped from the zoo.'

As soon as he had gone, I knocked on the kitchen window and waved at Marco to come back in.

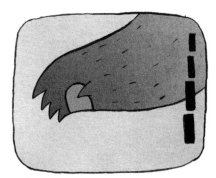

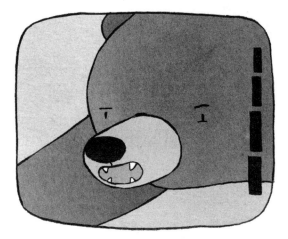

'That was quick thinking', I said.

'It was a bit too close for comfort, Patrick. It was touch and go. I almost didn't make it.'

'But you did make it, Marco. You were a perfect statue. You nearly had *me* convinced.'

'Thank you, Patrick.'

Every time I gave Marco a compliment, he said 'thank you'. Which was nice.

Being a statue must have made Marco thirsty, because he filled a pint glass with water from the tap and drank it down in one huge bear gulp. Then we went back in to watch the rest of the football game.

No sooner had we settled into the sofa than there was another ring on the doorbell.

'Stay there,' I said to Marco. 'Whoever it is, they won't be coming in here.'

How wrong I was.

FULL NAME
RUDOLPH KEARNS

DATE OF BIRTH
21/10/1975

ID NUMBER
021116030902

LICENCE INSPECTION

'TV Licence Inspector,' announced a smartly-dressed man, showing me a card with his picture on it. 'You have a television on the premises. I can hear it from here. Our records show that your licence was due for renewal six months ago. I will have to see the TV in question.'

I tried to put him off, but he was very pushy, and before I knew it he was through the front door and heading for the living room. This time I thought the game was up.

'Sorry, missus, for disturbing you,' the licence inspector said. 'Just having a look at the TV.'

Marco was curled up on the sofa with a large orange blanket over him. On his head was a huge floppy hat, a super-size one that someone had left behind on Pooka Beach. The moment Mum had seen it lying on the sand she knew it would be perfect for Marco.

'Actually,' I said to the inspector, 'Granddad gets very upset when anyone calls him "missus". Just because he wears a big floppy hat doesn't mean he's a she.'

The inspector looked embarrassed. His pushiness had disappeared.

'Of course not,' he said, looking down at Marco. 'I'm terribly sorry, sir.'

Marco started to snore. I was sure he was messing, but after I'd told the inspector that Mum would put the licence money in the post and had shown him to the door, I returned to the TV room to discover that he was fast asleep beneath the blanket and the floppy hat.

'Marco, wake up!'

'Ah Patrick, I was just about to catch a salmon. It was a lovely dream.'

I watched as he licked his bear lips. Then he threw off the blanket and stretched out on the sofa and let out an almighty yawn. In the five months he'd been living with us, I had never heard him yawn.

'I didn't know grizzlies yawned.'

'Patrick, there's a lot that you don't know about grizzlies. Anyway, I think I'll finish off the floor in the den. If I watch any more television I'll fall asleep again.'

Marco was a wizard when it came to carpentry. He had put up shelves in the kitchen. He'd made a beautiful desk for my bedroom, and now he was in the middle of laying a new wooden floor in the den.

He was only in the den ten minutes when the doorbell rang again.

'Chimney cleaner,' said a man in black overalls, his face covered in a fine coating of coal dust. 'Your mother rang me yesterday and told me to come round today, said you'd be here to let me in. Good lad.'

Before I had a chance to say 'Stop!' or 'MARCO!' he was through the door with all his chimney cleaning stuff and heading for the den. I couldn't believe this was happening. Why didn't Mum tell me he was coming?

'I'll start in here,' he called back to me. 'Your mother said to start in the den.'

'NO!'

Too late. He was already through the door. I hung my head in disbelief and helplessness. There was no escape for Marco because there was only one door into the den.

I waited for the shout of fright from the chimney cleaner and for the sound of him dropping his gear, followed by his flight from the room.

Instead, I heard his voice, loud and clear.

'That's a magnificent wall hanging! Never saw anything like it. Reminds me a little of the grizzly bear that escaped from the zoo.'

Wall hanging? What was he talking about?

I tiptoed down the hall and poked my head in through the open door. Marco had hung himself on the wall opposite the fireplace, his belly against the wall, his great big hairy back facing out into the room.

We live in an old house and all the rooms have high ceilings with a plaster border six inches from the ceiling. This was what Marco was clinging to with his claws.

'I'd better cover this up with a sheet,' the chimney cleaner said. 'Otherwise it might get coal dust all over it. And you don't want that now, do you, son?'

'No, sir.'

I ran upstairs to the hot press and pulled out the biggest sheet we had.

The chimney cleaner stood on a chair and draped it over Marco.

Before he was completely covered, I leaned against the wall to have a look at how he was doing. I reckoned it must have been difficult hanging on like that.

His eyes were closed, as if he was concentrating really hard, but he must have known I was looking

at him because he opened one eye, stared straight
at me, and winked.

That made two things in one day I had
discovered about grizzly bears: they could yawn
and they could wink. I never would have known
that.

I left the room and went in to watch TV. There was no point in worrying; Marco had everything under control. After about fifteen minutes, the chimney cleaner came into the living room and started to clean the chimney there.

While he was working, I went to the den to check on Marco. He was out for the count, Z a sleeping grizzly-bear-wall-hanging. He was z definitely a champion sleeper.

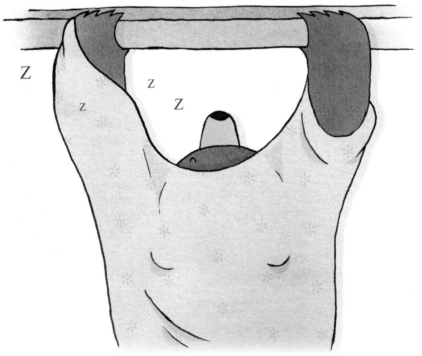

'You're having an interesting morning,' I said to him half-an-hour later, when the chimney cleaner was gone and we were both back in the living room.

'First you're a statue. Then you're my sleeping granddad. And finally you get to be a wall hanging. What a fascinating life you grizzly bears lead!'

I switched on the television. There was a programme about meerkats that Marco wanted to see. He just loved the way they would pop up suddenly as though they were listening for something, or standing guard. The floor in the den would have to wait.

Marco took his eyes off the screen for a moment.

'If it's alright with you, Patrick, I think I'd like the rest of the day to be nice and calm. Do you think you could organize that for me?'

We must have had the volume up really loud, because even Marco didn't hear Mr Frump come in, and Marco could usually hear a dog bark when no one else could. Maybe he was concentrating too hard on the meerkats.

But there he was, standing in the hall, looking in. I mustn't have closed the front door properly after the chimney cleaner left.

Mr Frump lived in the house across the road. He was a nice man who Mum had a soft spot for. He was very old and from May to September each year I'd call over every few weeks to cut his small front lawn with the old push mower he kept in his back shed.

Now that Marco was in our lives, I hadn't been going as often as I should. In fact, I'd only been there once, and that was nearly five weeks ago.

He was probably calling over to see what had happened to me.

His jaw had dropped open and he looked a little scared, which probably wasn't very healthy for such an old man.

'Oh my goodness! It's the grizzly bear that escaped from the zoo.'

Marco didn't move a muscle.

'Oh, hello, Mr Frump,' I said, as casually as I could. 'Do you want me to do your lawn?'

I honestly don't think he heard a word that I said. His feet appeared to be nailed to the floor. He was definitely in shock.

'It's the grizzly bear,' he said again, this time in a weaker voice.

'No it's not, Mr Frump. It may *look* like the grizzly bear that escaped from the zoo, but it's actually a robot.'

I jumped up from the sofa and went over to Mr Frump. I took him by the arm and brought him closer to Marco.

'Mr Frump, meet Marco, The Grizzly-Bear-Robot.'

'The **what**?'

'He's a robot, Mr Frump. Mum got him on loan from the Science Institute. He's an experiment. We've been chosen to try him out, to see what parts of him work, what parts don't.'

Mr Frump didn't seem convinced.

'Robots don't watch television,' he said.

Mr Frump may have been old, but he was no fool.

Robots don't watch TV.

'That's his Watching-TV position. When he isn't working, we can program him to sit and watch television with us, or to sit at the kitchen table while we're eating. Just to keep us company. But he doesn't talk. He's not a talking robot.'

'But what does a Grizzly-Bear-Robot *do*?'

I decided to give Mr Frump a demonstration.

'He's voice-activated. If I call out an instruction, he will carry it out. Watch.'

I put on what I thought sounded like a computer-generated voice.

'MARCO. TURN. OFF. TV'

Marco picked up the remote and pressed the OFF button.

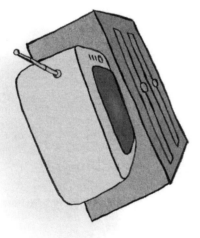

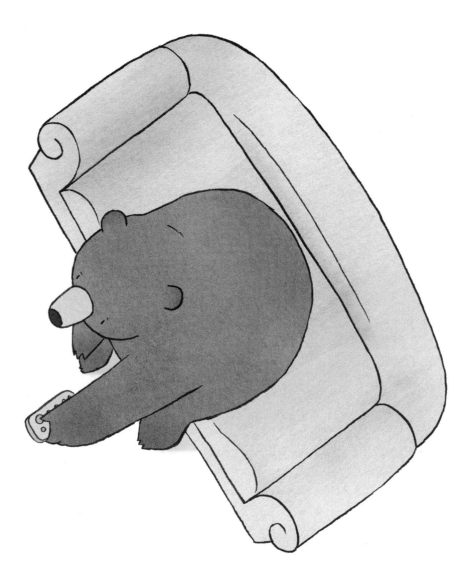

'MARCO. TAKE. HOOVER. FROM. CLOSET. HOOVER. HALL. CARPET.'

Mr Frump and I watched as Marco got up from the sofa and stood on his hind legs. Marco must have been watching science fiction B-movies in the mornings when I was at school; those really old movies with funny-looking robots who walk as if they are crippled with arthritis.

That's how Marco was moving. His arms and legs, and even his head and his neck moved in a jerky, awkward manner. Exactly like he thought a robot would move.

I felt his performance was a bit over the top, but Mr Frump lapped it up.

'My, my, my. Well, isn't that something? It's amazing what science can do nowadays, Patrick.'

'It certainly is, Mr Frump.'

By now Marco was in the hall, hoover in hand, hoovering like a robotic grizzly bear. He was brilliant!

Mr Frump went at last, but not before I had to show him how Marco made the beds, and how he chopped onions. I watched as he tottered towards the gate, repeating over and over, 'Well, wasn't that something? Wasn't that something?'

'What a crazy morning, Marco!'

Poor Marco. He was flopped on the sofa, the meerkats programme was over, and he looked exhausted.

'I know exactly what you need,' I said.

'A cup of tea?'

'Coming up, for MARCO, THE GRIZZLY-BEAR-ROBOT, a nice milky tea with no sugar.'

'Good man, Patrick. I don't know what I'd do without you.'

The doorbell rang **again**. I couldn't believe it. We *never* had this many visitors. Marco groaned. I looked out the window.

'It's one of those sales people, Marco. We won't bother answering it.'

Mum once said that if you let a door-to-door salesperson open their mouth, the only way to get them to stop is to buy something or shut the door in their face. She really hated them.

Marco was very fond of my mum. If Mum didn't like someone, Marco didn't like them either.

He gave me a strange look now, a look I hadn't seen before. His mouth twisted slightly and his eyes got smaller.

If I hadn't known it was Marco, I'd have been frightened.

'Open the door and invite him in,' he said.

'Are you **crazy**?'

'Trust me, Patrick. Open the door and invite the salesman in.'

'You're not going to break his arm or anything, are you?'

'The Two-Minute-Bear-Hug.'

'You're going to give him the Two-Minute-Bear-Hug? **The Two-Minute-Bear-Hug**?'

Soon after he came to stay with us, Marco told Mum and me about the hugging traditions in his family. There was the Five-Second-Hug, which was bear language for 'Hello, good to see you', and then the longer and longer hugs that meant all kinds of different things.

The longest hug Marco had given Mum and me was the One-Minute-Hug, which was meant to make you happy and full of energy. When you were in the hug, all you could see and smell was grizzly bear.

Even though you knew it would be over in a minute, it felt like it would never end. It was definitely not a pleasant experience, though we didn't tell Marco that.

It did make us feel a little happier, but not right away, because the hugging itself squeezed all the energy out of us and we both had to lie down for an hour to recover.

But we had never had the Two-Minute-Hug.

The Two-Minute-Hug was the longest bear hug of all. It was for a bear who had had a traumatic experience, like a death in the family, or a close shave with a hunter whose bullet missed him by inches.

The Two-Minute-Hug had a bit of real bear magic. As well as making you feel happier, it made you forget everything that had happened to you that day. You even forgot you got the hug. You walked away in a dream and you stayed like that for twenty-four hours.

And now Marco was going to give it to the salesman.

I opened the door.

'Hello there, young man. How are you today? Is your mother or your father at home?'

The salesman had a voice as smooth as silk. He was dressed in a dark green suit with a white shirt and a flowery tie. He had a wide smile on his suntanned face.

'Come in,' I said. 'My father would like to hug … sorry, would like to meet you.'

Marco was standing behind the door. When I closed it the salesman swivelled around to shake my father's hand.

In the split second it took him to see that it was not my father but an eight-foot tall grizzly bear, the blood drained right out of his face.

And then Marco began the Two-Minute- Hug.

When it was over, the salesman behaved as Marco had said he would. He looked suddenly much happier, and he had a dreamy expression on his face, like he was in a trance, which in a way he was. I opened the door and let him out and I watched as he floated – at least that's what it looked like – towards the gate.

'I wonder what his wife will think when he gets home,' I said to Marco.

'She'll probably like him better,' he said.

I thought that was a really wise thing to say, but then Marco often said very wise things.

'You are an amazing grizzly bear,' I said.

'Thank you, Patrick.'

'I think we both deserve a cup of tea after all that madness,' I said.

We walked down the hall towards the kitchen.

'Patrick?'

'Yes, Marco.'

'What do you think of the idea of me building a bigger shed in the back garden?'

'That's a brilliant idea.'

'I could make a start on it after I've had my cup of tea. You go put the kettle on. I'll have a look at the shed, make a few calculations, tell you how much wood to order. How does that sound?'

'Sounds good, Marco.'

'Let me know when the kettle is boiled,' he said, and he ambled out the back door and headed towards the shed.